Peter Goes to School

By Wanda Rogers House

Pictures by Hal W. Doremus

Giant Wonder Books®

PRICE STERN SLOAN

Los Angeles

TODAY IS THE DAY. Today is the day Peter has been waiting for. Today is the day Peter goes to school!

Every morning Peter has asked his mother, "Is *this* the day I go to school?"

Every night Peter has asked his father, "Is *to-morrow* the day I go to school?"

Now tomorrow is today. Peter doesn't understand how that can be. But just the same, tomorrow is today now.

And *today* is the day Peter goes to school.

"Time to get dressed," Mother calls. "Time to get dressed for school!"

Mother gives Peter his corduroy overalls and striped shirt.

"These will be just right to play in. These will be just right for school."

Peter helps Mother get breakfast. Peter eats every bit of his cereal, but he doesn't drink all his milk.

Not this morning! This morning Peter is too busy thinking about school.

"Never mind," says Mother. "At school you will have milk to drink. This morning you may wait and drink your milk with the other children at school."

Peter knows just where his school is. He knows
what his school looks like on the *outside*.

But he doesn't know at all what it looks like
on the *inside*. That's why Peter is holding tight to
Mother's hand.

There are steps up to the doors of school. Mother and Peter go up the steps. Step, step, step—up the steps to school.

They open the big doors to Peter's school. Peter holds tight to Mother's hand.

All at once Peter isn't at all sure that he wants to go to school. All at once Peter wants to go back home with Mother.

Children often feel like that about new things and new places. Even big children. Even Peter.

Inside Peter's school, music is playing. The children are having a parade!

One boy beats a drum. Another boy is tapping with tap sticks. And a little girl with ribbons in her hair is jingling silver wrist bells.

Peter watches the children parade.

March, march, go their feet around the red tables, and around the blue chairs. March, go their feet past the block shelves, and past the sand table. MARCH, MARCH, MARCH!

Peter sees the doll corner with the doll bed and
the ironing board. Peter sees the shelves full of
trucks and tractors and cars. There are cupboards
of crayons and paper and clay. There are puzzles
and peg sets and easels and paint.

"I want to go parading, too!" shouts Peter.

Mother helps Peter hang up his coat and hat.

There is one drum left for Peter. Now Peter can parade, too.

BOOM, BOOM, goes Peter's drum. March, march, go Peter's feet.

"Good-by, Mother," calls Peter. "I am going to parade!"

"Good-by, Peter," smiles Mother. "When you come home, tell me about the parade."

When the music stops, the children are ready for milk and crackers. The milk is in stiff paper containers. There is a cracker to eat with the milk.

Peter holds his container very straight so the milk won't spill.

The girl with ribbons in her hair forgets. Tip, goes her container! Splish, splash, goes the milk!

"Never mind," says the teacher. "It was an accident."

The girl with the ribbons gets a cloth and wipes the spot away.

"Good work," smiles the teacher.

Then the teacher says, "After our rest, we will go outdoors to play. Now it is time to lie down on our mats."

There is a mat for each child. There is a mat for Peter, too.

The children lie quietly with their eyes closed. Peter is so busy looking at all the toys and all the children that he forgets to close his eyes. Next time, Peter will close his eyes, too.

Out in the yard at school, there are swings and a slide, and a tricycle to ride.

There are ladders to climb on, and boxes to build a house to play in.

There is a barrel to roll, and a long, low plank to walk across.